QUIT
STRONG
WOMAN

RAVINDER KAUR

ISBN 978-1-68487-115-5

Dedicated to

All the strong women in the world...

Contents

Foreword

Success & Failure, Happiness & Sadness in life is directly related to how we experience relationships, which has the power to either disempower or make us emerge stronger!

This book will pave the way to push everyone in the right direction.

It feels great to know someone like Ms. Ravinder Kaur, who's a wonderful soul. Her truly inspiring work as an Author has transformed lives around. Being a Life & Relationship Coach and an Author myself, I duly feel the importance of guiding someone in their personal life and the huge impact just one piece of advice can create.

I feel privileged to write this Foreword as I firmly believe in the 'Power of Women', something Ms. Ravinder is going to help you 'Rediscover within You'. Reading this book itself will 'Unleash Your Power' and forge ahead on your 'Path to Prosperity.

I feel lucky to have this book with you right now, as you embark upon a new journey...

Sandeep Bogra

India's Best Life & Relationship Coach
2x Bestselling Author

Acknowledgements

I am highly grateful to you as you are holding this book in your hands. No achievement, big or small, is possible without the support of one's family, friends, and Almighty. It would not have been possible without the support of many people.

My family has always been special to me, my mother and father have been a great source of inspiration in my life. They have been encouraging me to chase my dreams.

I am also thankful to my husband Bharpur (my source of strength) for his full support and assistance. I want to thank my husband for loving me the way I am, for being smart & supporting me 100% which made this book possible.

I am indebted to everyone who directly or indirectly shaped my life, encouraged me, criticized me, and ultimately made me what I am and where I am today. I am greatly thankful to all whom I met along the way. I am obliged to Sweta Samota, Amazon Bestselling Author, Motivational Speaker, and ChangeMaker who changed my life to a great extent and shared various nuggets of writing.

Last but not the least, I would like to thank the Almighty. He supports me every time I am stuck with words. My belief in God helped me to go the extra mile towards a new life.

CHAPTER ONE

Day 1

The beautiful chirping sounds of the birds; early in the morning woke up Shalini; stretching her arms; she got up from her bed; drew the curtains to view the beautiful orange rising sun from the balcony of her bedroom. It was a routine since her life took a drastic change due to some bitter life experiences. She used to come to the balcony for a few minutes and stare at the sun to feel how the Sun looks so beautiful and new every day and how it would change her day with a new hope. After spending ten minutes in the balcony, she went to the kitchen to prepare green tea; enjoyed sipping while sitting in the balcony and started reading the newspaper. She took up the diary to write something new that she was doing for the last twenty-five years.

After spending time with diary, sharing feelings and dumping them on her second close friend (diary) after Ankita, she went to Ankita's room to wake her up.

"Good morning, Ankita," she kissed on her forehead.

"Good morning."

Ankita covered her face with her arms as Shalini drew the curtains.

"It's Sunday, ten minutes more please."

"I know all of your daily dialogues since childhood. Please act like a mature one. You are going to be twenty-six not sweet sixteen, dear. Get up and be ready. I am going to prepare breakfast for us, see you at the table. Come in fifteen minutes. Waiting for you there."

"Comminnng, Mom," Ankita spoke lazily.

Ankita pulled the sheets to cover her face and wanted to sleep for more as her inner childish behaviour wanted to stay more in the bed. How did her fifteen minutes turn into one hour? She realised it when her alarm piece rang up suddenly at 8 a.m. This day of the week, sweet Sunday gives her a unique relaxation. She wanted to start her Sunday in her way. She got up from her bed, set her beautiful but entangled hair with her long, soft fingers, and clipped them with a hair clutcher placed on the bedside table.

After getting ready, Ankita went to the dining table. Shalini was arranging cutlery on the dining table for breakfast.

"I am ready, Mom," Ankita hugged her mom tightly from the back.

As they were having breakfast, Shalini started a conversation with Ankita, "I have a surprise for you."

"Not again, Mom, please."

"No more marriage proposal, please," Ankita continued with frown eyebrows.

"Listen Ankita," Shalini continued, "Yesterday I got a call from a decent family and they wanted to see you first; so, I invited them today for the meeting."

"How could you do that, Mom?"

"At least discuss with me before finalising anything."

"Listen, listen Ankita. We didn't finalise anything. They wanted to meet you. So, I thought you would be free from the hospital and Sunday would be suitable for all."

"Mom you are too much."

"But you are more than too much beta," Shalini smiled and hugged her again.

Suddenly the phone rang, Shalini worriedly questioned her, "No, not this time, please."

"Mom, how could you forget that I am a doctor and my priority is my patients? It might be an emergency else they would never call."

As Ankita answered the call from the hospital, she hurriedly moved to the hospital; informing Shalini to make sure that the family she had invited to postpone their plans to some other day.

"Every time you do this," responded Shalini with frown eyes.

Shalini went to her room and again started writing in her diary; she jotted down all her feelings in her diary and the doorbell rang suddenly.

"Ding Dong."

She moved towards the door; rotated the knob of the main door and here was her maid, Sheela. She wore a cotton dark blue coloured printed saree with her hairs pinned up in a bun. She had been working there for the last two years.

"Namaste, Mam," Sheela wished Shalini and entered the house.

She started cleaning utensils and started talking with Shalini.

Being in conversation with her maid Sheela, Shalini forgot to inform the family who wanted to come to see Ankita.

CHAPTER TWO

The Same Day @ Rohan's Home

Rohan's family was getting ready and was about to leave. Rohan was the only son of his parents. His parents were curious to meet Ankita and wanted to know about her. They started assuming her with their point of view. Rohan's parents were discussing that their only son who never woke up early before on Sunday has changed a lot since we started his talks with Ankita.

Mrs. Gupta shared her feelings with her husband, "I have been noticing him since we started his talks with Ankita's family."

Rohan was not at home; he was at the car washing centre as he planned for that in advance. It took around two hours at the car washing centre. He reached home around 11 a.m. with his newly serviced car.

He had breakfast before leaving for Panchkula, where they planned to see the girl, Ankita. He went in his car and started practicing in his mind what he would say when he meets Ankita. How would he start his conversation with Ankita? He started speaking in his mind till his parents arrived.

"Hi! I am Rohan Gupta, a known lawyer of the city fighting social evils cases. I am very confident in the courtroom. But today I am nervous like I am going to sit for

UPSC exam as seeing a girl for a marriage proposal was not less than an exam of life for me."

Suddenly he heard a knock on the window of the driver's seat. His parents were asking him to open the door. As his parents were seated in the car, he asked the address and followed the shortest route as he was equally curious to see Ankita. Rohan was in his imagination, assuming the girl, her colour, voice, and her style on the way to her home.

As they reached the Ankita's apartment, they took the lift to the eighth floor where Ankita was staying with her mother. The view of their apartment was breathtaking. Rohan was curious to see Ankita. The heartbeat of Rohan was ten steps ahead of him. He was cross-fingered.

They rang the doorbell.

"Ding Dong ...."

Sheela was mopping the floor.

"Sheela, please check who is at the door," Shalini commanded Sheela.

Sheela opened the door.

"Whom do you want to meet?" questioned Sheela.

Rohan was curious to get inside the home to meet Ankita. But the maidservant was having a long list of questions. Rohan requested his father to call Ms. Shalini Mehra.

Suddenly, a sweet voice came from one of the rooms.

"Sheela, who is at the door?"

"Mam, Guptas have come to meet you," replied Sheela quickly.

"Sheela, please make them sit in the drawing-room and offer them water. I am coming," Shalini spoke in the same sweet voice.

Rohan was stunned to see the interior of the drawing-room. On the east wall of the drawing-room, there was beautiful floral canvas hanging, adding beauty to the drawing-room. Rohan sat in front of that canvas and his parents sat in front of his sofa. Within a few seconds, a lady in a green silk saree with pearl jewellery came with folded hands. She was showing our beautiful Indian culture in her dressing style.

Rohan was very curious to see Ankita. But his imagination was swirling at the speed of the airplane as he saw Ankita's mother. He couldn't keep his eyes away from her mother.

"Namaste, myself Shalini Mehra."

"Nice to meet you all."

Hope you found our location in no time. You know the roundabouts of Chandigarh look the same and can confuse anyone," Shalini continued.

"No, I am used to these roads," smiled Rohan.

"We talked yesterday about our children's marriage proposal," asked Mr Gupta.

"But first I want to see you and want to discuss something about my family," Shalini whispered.

Rohan was so impressed with Shalini's voice, that he again went into his dream girl's imagination. He was comparing Ankita's mom and Ankita in his dreams. He was imagining her from every point, her style, voice, colour, and looks. Suddenly a voice came and he came to his senses.

"Rohan Beta, I think I should have informed you in the morning that Ankita will be busy today as she has an emergency in the hospital. So sorry, you cannot meet her today. But as I scheduled our meeting for today, I don't want to let it go in vain," informed Shalini.

"I think this is the right time I can discuss with you everything about my life."

Mrs. Gupta interrupted, "My son, Rohan Gupta is practising Law for two years. I know you may be getting more proposals for your daughter. He is our only son and we will treat Ankita as our daughter."

Shalini repeated, "I know you would. But I had something else to share with you. I don't want to keep anything secret from you; just let me share my point."

Mr and Mrs Gupta raised their eyebrows and allowed her to continue her discussion,

Shalini sighed deeply and started her story with patience.

That was a time when I was in Jaipur for a four-day college trip with my college friends. I met Anish, a professor in one of the private colleges of Jaipur with their students on a one-day college trip. I was in Jaipur with my classmates. I was impressed by his genuine charming behaviour. On his one-day trip, he shared his WhatsApp number with me and we started chatting and within hours our chatting converted into video calls and our relationship changed to a great extent.

He called me to be with him on our visit to Amer Fort, the famous tourist spot of Jaipur; constructed with red stones and marbles. He explained to us the minutest details of Amer Fort as he had been working there as a part-time tourist guide. He explained to us that the fort is divided into four levels - Diwan-e-Aam, Diwan-e-Khas, Sheesh Mahal and Sukh Niwas. He was very keen to guide us about all the historical connections of Amer Fort and its layout. It took four hours to cover the Amer Fort.

After the Amer Fort, he advised our college teachers to visit Sanjay Museum and Albert Museum. It looked like he wanted to spend more time with me. The whole day went in Amer Fort, Sanjay Museum and Albert Museum. The night view of the colour changing Albert Museum amazed all. We were tired after a hectic day and decided to leave for the hotel.

The next day, we had breakfast in the hotel and left for some more tourist attraction spots such as Gatore Ki Chattaryian, Hawa Mahal, City Palace and Jantar Mantar. After our four days stay at Jaipur, when I was back in Panchkula, I wrote a letter to Anish to proceed with our relation to the next step. He was damn sure of our marriage. But when I discussed my news of pregnancy with him after the confirmation by doctors, he denied proceeding with this pregnancy. I tried my best to convince him but he never wanted this child. Somewhere he was not sure whether he could convince his parents or not.

He was not in contact with me for two months. Then, I decided to start a new journey as I was damn sure of his intentions. Then I never called him back. I blocked him from all social media. But I proceeded with my pregnancy and delivered a beautiful daughter, Ankita. Twenty-five years ago, it was a tough time for me to become a single mother. That was the most horrible part of my journey and it transformed me a lot to start my life with Ankita with a new hope.

Once I tried to share with Ankita about her father when she was just ten years old but she never liked to listen about her father. So, I never discussed anything about Anish. That's all about me. I am a single mother. But still, in India, single mothers are never respected. I made her a doctor and handed over the management of my parents' hospital to her. Ankita will take care of my parents' property.

"I wanted to clear my point with you before proceeding further. Rest depends upon you, after all, it's your as well as Rohan's decision," concluded Shalini.

Sheela came with the cups of tea kept in a white floral rectangular tray and served everyone with biscuits and snacks.

Rohan was in a dilemma about what to say next; he just glared at his parents and was noticing the reaction of all. After a few seconds, Mrs Gupta requested Shalini to give them some time to think.

After drinking tea, when they were about to leave, Rohan asked Shalini, "Can I meet Ankita if you don't mind?" Shalini stood still but after a few seconds, she gave her consent and address of her hospital to Rohan.

"But promise me, you will not share anything with her that we discussed today," Shalini pleaded.

"You can trust me," Rohan assured.

CHAPTER THREE

Day 2

Rohan was eager to meet Ankita, he was unable to sleep; he was in the dreams of Ankita. A series of questions was vacillating in his mind.

"How will I meet her?"

"How will she react?"

"Will she be comfortable when I meet?"

"Whether I should go or not?"

The whole night went with the long list of questions and the only answer was to sleep now. Otherwise, he would be late for tomorrow's meeting.

He set an alarm for 6 o'clock at 2:00 a.m. He slept just for four hours. He followed his routine and got himself ready by 8:00 a.m. as he planned to leave for the hospital to meet Ankita.

He came out of his room and sat on the dining table to have breakfast. He called her mom and requested her to serve him first as he was in a hurry and was going to meet Ankita. His mother started preaching to him, "Don't ask her any irrelevant courtroom questions. It should be your casual meet."

"Oh! Mom, come on," cried Rohan.

"Do you think I am still a kid?" Rohan asked while eating bread toast wrapped with peanut butter.

"Mom, please just stop this now, don't change my mood, I am not in the mood to listen. It would be better if we discuss this later on," Rohan requested his mom.

He had his breakfast and moved hurriedly out of his home to get in the car. Suddenly, his mind signaled that he forgot his wallet in his room, he came out of his car and rushed towards his room to collect his wallet.

He had just entered his home when his mother questioned, "What happened?"

He again shouted, "Only because of you, I forgot my wallet in the room and left in a hurry. I am already late, Mom."

He picked up his wallet and set his hair in front of the oval-shaped classic design mirror installed on the wall of the room.

He talked in front of the mirror feeling happy and excited, "I am coming, Ankita."

He again got in the car and started to move towards Ankita's hospital. He turned on the stereo; it made him happier; his favourite song was on the playlist. He started singing the song along with the singer like *Zara Zara Behakta Hai, Mehakta Hai Aaj To Mera Tan Badan...* He closed the window panes of his car and sang the song aloud. This was his favourite song; it made his day a romantic start. He reached the red-light point, a beggar came and knocked at his window, he scrolled down the windowpane and gave him Rs. 50.

The beggar gave him the blessing, "May God bless you with all the happiness!"

As the signal turned to green, he started towards the hospital, then he saw a traffic jam near to the hospital and he scrolled down the windowpane and asked from the passersby, "What happened?" The passerby nodded his head and showed his hand to wait till the road jam get cleared.

He waited for ten minutes till the jam cleared and finally, he reached the hospital. He parked his car at the parking lot and left for the reception counter. There was a crowd of emergency cases on Monday. A queue of 15-17 people was there at the reception counter to receive the token number for their OPD consultation. Rohan went directly to the receptionist.

"Hello mam, I am Rohan, I want to meet Dr. Ankita," Rohan asked the receptionist.

The receptionist asked, "Do you have any appointment with her?"

"No, I am Rohan, please tell her I am here to meet her for a personal reason. She will understand."

The receptionist dialed Dr. Ankita's number and explained about Rohan, "Dr. Ankita, Mr. Rohan has come to meet you but he has no appointment for today."

Ankita informed the receptionist, "Tell him to wait."

The receptionist informed him to sit in the waiting room.

Rohan asked the receptionist, "Where is the waiting room?"

The receptionist signaled him towards the waiting room. Rohan went there and started reading magazines placed on the side table. He was just turning the pages as he was in no mood to read them. He was waiting for the receptionist's call.

Ankita called her mother to enquire about Rohan, "Why has he come here to meet me? Mom, why did you give him the address of my hospital?" Ankita continued her questions one after another.

Shalini requested her daughter, "Please calm down and talk to him as he is not there to propose you; he just wanted to meet you as you were not there yesterday when he came with his parents to our home."

Ankita was finally convinced by her mother's words and called at the reception to let him come in.

Rohan got up from the sofa and walked towards Ankita's room. The receptionist waved her hand towards the left side. He just took a left turn from the reception counter and saw Room No. 101 with the nameplate, Dr. Ankita. He knocked at the door, a sweet voice came, "Please, come in."

He held his breath and entered her cabin. The room was very spacious and was stuffed with the fragrance of Lavender flowers. He was mesmerized by the beauty of Dr. Ankita. She was just like a princess of her father, with long black hair, deep dark brown eyes and the beautiful shape of her lips made him hypnotized.

He was not in his senses. Ankita told him to have a seat but he was lost in his dreams.

She called Rohan but no response came.

Then she again called him, "Rohan, what happened?"

She went to him; shook his shoulder and he was back in his senses. Ankita asked, "Any problem, Rohan?"

He stepped back and fixed his gaze at her.

She again offered, "Please have a seat, Rohan."

He pulled the chair back and stood in front of Ankita and asked her, "Ladies always first. Please sit, Ankita."

Ankita sat on her chair and advised him to sit; so, they could start their talks.

She asked, "What would you like to have, tea or coffee?"

"I only want a glass of water as I have a dry throat after waiting for you," replied Rohan.

She smiled after this and set her hair behind her ears with long fingers.

She put off the table coaster and offered the glass of water to Rohan which was already kept on her table.

"Thank you, Ankita"

"Welcome, Rohan. It is my pleasure. Can you please introduce yourself so that we can start our conversation?"

"Hi, I am Rohan Gupta, a known lawyer of the city; fighting the cases to remove the social evils. I hope your mother told you the reason why I am here."

She nodded her head and smiled, "What do you want to know about me?"

Then she introduced herself, "I am Dr. Ankita Mehra, a gynecologist. Do you want to know anything specific about me?"

"Could you please spare thirty minutes for our meeting outside the hospital if you feel free for this, right now or when you feel comfortable? I hope you don't mind. If you have some emergency then we can plan for some other day. I am not in a hurry. You take your time, I'll wait for you outside at the reception," demanded Rohan.

She started looking at the window and thinking about Rohan's plan. He stood up and reminded her to think about his proposal for coffee only.

She laughed genuinely and told him to sit and wait inside the cabin and let her discuss with the receptionist if there were any appointments within two hours.

He stood up and walked towards the window and started surfing on his mobile.

She informed the receptionist, "Please, allocate all my appointments and emergencies to Dr. Ishaan. I will be back within an hour or two. Check with Dr. Ishaan and send him to my cabin right now."

The receptionist informed Dr. Ishaan that Dr. Ankita is calling him in her cabin.

Suddenly, someone knocked at the door.

"Come in, Dr. Ishaan."

"Good morning doctor."

She continued, "I would not be available for an hour."

"Could you handle all my appointments in my absence?" Ankita continued.

"Sure," replied Dr. Ishaan.

"Any problem Dr. Ankita? You can share with me," questioned Dr. Ishaan.

"No problem as such. Thanks for your concern, Dr. Ishaan."

"You are always welcomed."

Dr. Ishaan went towards the door; opened the door and left. He went to the receptionist to check for Dr. Ankita's appointments for the day. The receptionist opened today's appointment folder from the desktop and started searching for Dr. Ankita's appointments which were scheduled within two hours. She sent the details of the appointments on Dr. Ishaan's mobile. As Dr. Ishaan turned, he saw Dr. Ankita with a person, who was unknown to him and was shocked about him.

Who is he?

Why is he with Ankita?

Where did he come from?

Dr. Ishaan's mind created several surprising and mind-boggling questions about that person.

Ankita was holding her handbag in one hand and her mobile in the other. She stopped at the reception to inform the receptionist to call her in case any emergency came.

Dr. Ishaan assured Dr. Ankita, "I will manage all your appointments for two hours. It is only a matter of two hours. So, don't worry. I will manage it."

"You can call me anytime in case of emergency."

"Sure, Dr. Ankita."

Then Rohan and Ankita left the hospital.

"Wait here, Ankita. Let me bring my car from the parking lot."

"I think I should take my car too." This was the sweet voice of Ankita. Rohan turned back.

"Any problem, Ankita."

"No, not at all. Otherwise, you have to drop me again at the hospital. So, I think I should take my car too."

"I would feel happy to drop you here. This time would give me a chance to know more about you. So, I think, I should grab this chance."

"Okay," nodded Ankita.

He parked the car near Ankita; came out of the car; opened the door for her and requested her to sit inside. As, she sat in the car, she smiled and thanked Rohan. He closed the door softly; and moved to his side to sit in the car and drove the car towards the café.

Both were sitting quietly and were waiting for each other to start.

He switched on the car stereo and started playing romantic songs.

She taunted him, "Are you trying to impress me? I am not that kind of girl. I am a simple girl and love simplicity."

After listening to her words, Rohan muted the car stereo.

Rohan glanced at her as she was busy surfing on her mobile.

He interrupted her, "Please stop this surfing; share something more about you so we could know each other better than before. I am not that boring that you have to surf on mobile!"

"Oh! I didn't mean that. I am sorry if you are hurt in any way."

"By the way, where are we going for coffee?"

"Ankita, you suggest your favourite café."

"Please don't waste time in deciding; you have given me time constraints," he glanced at his wrist.

"May I ask you a personal question?" questioned Ankita.

"Huh! A personal one."

"Why not?" replied Rohan.

"I didn't mean that, I mean something about your professional life." she clarified.

"Oh! It's so boring," he whispered.

"I mean about your today's commitment to court," confirmed Ankita.

"I took a day off from my professional duties," Rohan declared.

"But I don't think you need to take a day off for the coffee."

"Nothing like that."

"I just wanted to spend time with you to know you better."

"Sorry, Rohan."

"You should have informed me before, as I had made a lot of commitments in the hospital. We should have planned for some other day."

He got angry; took a U-turn and drove fast towards the hospital.

"What happened Rohan?" she questioned but there was pin-drop silence in the car.

He drove quietly and applied brakes at the hospital door.

He came out of the car and opened the door for Ankita, she came out, but was expecting Rohan to speak something.

They both kept quiet and moved to their respective ways. As Rohan sat in the car, he saw Ankita's mobile. He called her from the car, "Ankita, Ankita... listen. You forgot your mobile in my car."

The loud voice of Rohan compelled the gatekeeper to come near him and asked him to give the mobile; he would hand it over to Dr. Ankita.

Rohan left the hospital and waited for one day for her call.

He was furious at her behaviour. He had never expected this from her. He was waiting for her call or message. He was checking his mobile after every minute whether it is in the network area or the signal problem is there. He forgot that he has not given her his number. But he was having her number.

He sent a "Sorry" text to Ankita. She ignored the message as it was from an unknown number. After fifteen minutes, she got a series of messages from the same number.

She ignored all the messages and left the hospital in the evening. When Rohan got no replies so finally, he got the courage to call her and apologize for his awkward behaviour that hurt her a lot. Rohan gave her a call but she was already upset because of the person who was sending her messages since afternoon.

Rohan called her for the second time, she picked and started shouting at the person on the other end.

"Who are you?"

"Why are you sending me 'Sorry' messages?"

"Don't you have any other task to do?"

"I would register a complaint against you."

"Ankita please control, it's me, Rohan. We met in the morning."

"Oh, Rohan! It's you teasing me, since afternoon. By the way, how did you get my number, did you get my number from the receptionist?"

She started knitting stories, "How you got my number?" She was surprised.

"Wait, Ankita. You just relax and calm down. There is nothing like that," Rohan answered politely and explained his part, "I got your number when you forgot your mobile in the car. Then I gave ring to my number from yours. Sorry, if you didn't like my way, my intention was very clear to me to apologise to you."

As he concluded his part, she got a parallel call from the hospital. She held Rohan's call and asked him to wait, "I have to attend to the call from the hospital, there might be an emergency."

She attended the call from the hospital and accidentally Rohan's call gets disconnected.

Rohan started whispering behind her call that she stayed busy throughout.

Will she get time for him?

She went to the hospital after the call and kept busy the whole day.

As she was returning from the hospital. She thought "Oh! I forgot about Rohan's call as I left his call accidentally." She picked her phone while driving; opened the contacts list; searched for the unknown number and dialed that number. His number was out of coverage. She tried for one more time and she got the same message again ("The number you are trying to reach is busy, please try again later.")

Ankita called him in the evening as he was walking in his garden. Suddenly his heart started beeping rapidly with the expectation of her call. They both apologized for their awkward behaviour simultaneously.

"Sorry, Ankita."

"Sorry, Rohan."

They started laughing together.

"Leave all things behind; let's start a new journey with a new introduction," Rohan confessed.

"Okay, Rohan."

Their discussion lasted for twenty minutes and he was seeking a positive reply from her; so, he crossed his fingers and jumped after her reply. They finalised their first date on the day after tomorrow i.e., Thursday (15th August) as it was the off day for both. They both disconnected the call thereafter.

CHAPTER FOUR

14ᵗʰ August, 10:00 p.m.

Ankita and Rohan were eager for their first date, but they didn't get time to plan because of their busy schedule. They didn't even get time to chat with each other. They both dialed each other's number but it was giving a busy tone from both sides as both were trying to call each other at the same time. After ten minutes, Ankita's number gets connected with Rohan and she starts with a series of questions.

"Where were you busy?"

"I was trying for the last fifteen minutes and it was giving a busy tone."

Rohan interrupted her in between, calmed her down, and requested her to listen to his part first. She stopped and requested him to continue with his story, a new knitted one.

He pleaded her not to tease him again and again for the same.

"Ok, let me tell you the reason. I was also trying your number but your number was also busy."

"Where were you busy?"

"Now, you tell me your knitted stories."

"Confess me, Ankita."

"Where were you busy when I was busy too?"

"I think we should leave the matter of sorry and thank you as in our 'Sorry.... Thank You, Sorry.... Thank You,' we will not get time to know each other," he finalised.

"Yes, of course," she smiled.

She offered him to start with his part as she was very tired due to her hectic schedule, nothing was in her mind to start with.

"I don't know where to start?"

"I don't know how to start?"

"What should I say?"

"As my tired mind is not giving me any signal. If you don't mind then can we start our chat tomorrow?"

"Of course, Dr. Saab as you wish," he replied.

They wished each other good night and disconnected their call. Ankita was so tired that she went to sleep within ten minutes. On the other hand, Rohan was feeling restless; he was changing his position on the bed as he was trying to get a good night sleep for a better morning. But it took him three to four hours to sleep. Finally, he slept at 2 o'clock while surfing on his mobile.

CHAPTER FIVE

15th August @ Rohan's Home

He woke up with the mobile alarm. He was shocked to see the time as he was too late; the time was already 8 o'clock. He had planned the coffee date with Ankita at 10 o'clock. He followed his routine hurriedly; he had his breakfast; opened the almirah for choosing the clothes. But he was a little confused about what to wear; what not to wear; which colour suited him best; he was thinking about her favourite colour as he didn't know about her likes and dislikes. Their chat always started with Sorry and Thank You and always ended with Sorry and Thank You. They never got time to know about each other. He promised himself that he would try his best to know her better today itself. He would not give her a chance to say Sorry and Thank You.

He randomly took his black jeans with a white shirt as he used to wear them casually. He chose to wear dark brown colour sports shoes.

He took the keys and called Ankita to be ready, "I would pick you from your apartment. I will give you a ring when I am there."

CHAPTER SIX

15th August @ Ankita's Home

Ankita was baffled too as she was fussy. She took all the dresses out of her wardrobe and started trying in front of her room wall mirror. She tried pink, yellow, green, and blue but with so much confusion in mind she finally picked up lemon kurta with blue leggings.

She opened her accessories box to match the earrings and a bracelet. She was ready within 10 minutes. She was coming down the stairs to have breakfast, her mobile rang up suddenly.

'This is Rohan's call.'

She refused her mother for breakfast as Rohan was waiting for her in the car near the apartment gate. Ankita's mother advised her, "Call Rohan upstairs and you both can have breakfast here."

"Mom, how can he come as we have planned a coffee date today? I would give your message to him."

"Ok, as you wish," replied Ankita's mom.

She left in a hurry; called him to wait as she was in the lift and no network would be there in that area.

She reached near to his car; he gently opened the door for Ankita.

"Thanks, Rohan." She sat in the car; kept her mobile in the car front dashboard; wore a seat belt.

Rohan started his car and Ankita was curious to know where they were going for a coffee.

"Where you wanna go for a coffee? We can go to one of your favourite ones," Rohan questioned.

Ankita wished to go to his favourite coffee house this time. Then Rohan suggested, "There is a Costa Coffee in VR."

He followed the route to Mohali airport road which was directly linked with VR. It was the best route for the long drive. This time, she turned on the car stereo. As usual, the romantic songs were in a queue.

"You only love romantic songs," asked Ankita with her raised eyebrows.

"Yes, I have a very boring professional life so to keep myself energetic and happy I listen to these songs."

"Oh! Okay."

After a twenty-five minutes' drive on Airport Road, they went to VR, Rohan parked his car in the basement parking zone. They took the lift and pressed the UG button for Costa Coffee. Rohan ordered two hot coffees as they reached there.

They took two seats for them and started talking till the time they got their order.

"Do you think I am a boring person?" asked Ankita.

"I can't comment till you start talking. All our discussion usually starts with Sorry and Thank you so I don't want to comment on anything."

Their order came and they held their coffee mugs in their hands and were feeling the aroma of the coffee.

"What do you want to know about me?" asked Ankita while sipping her coffee.

"What do you think your friend should know about you? It's your choice, I am not forcing you about anything," replied Rohan.

Ankita thought for a while and whispered, "I had a past."

Rohan laughed, "If it was your past then why are you so desperate to share with me as you are going to be my future. What matters is our future and not your past, so focus on our future."

"Our means???" asked Ankita.

He reminded her, "We are friends now. So, the future will be ours. It was only my decision to meet you before proceeding further."

They had their coffee and started window shopping in the mall.

"Do you think we should ask our parents to discuss our marriage or do you need some time to think?" questioned Rohan.

"Give me some time to think as we are not getting married only; two families are going to be mingled. Let me discuss with my mom then I will call you in the evening," Ankita continued.

"You should take your time."

Rohan went home after dropping Ankita at her home and reminded her to discuss their matter with her mother.

"I know your mom's decision," this reply of his amazed Ankita.

"What do you mean? How do you know?" asked Ankita.

"We discussed all the matter the day we came to your place. But I decided to meet you before finalising anything."

"OMG! So, the only decision depends on me."

She raised her eyebrows.

"What do you think would be my answer?" she smiled.

"As I know you till date, it would be the best decision of your life,"

"Very confident!" Ankita exclaimed.

"I know my choice," Rohan replied.

They both waved hands and Ankita went inside the lift.

Rohan took his way home.

As he reached home, he started screaming, "Mom, Dad! Where are you? I have a surprise."

"What happened? You are very happy today. Did you propose her?" asked Mrs. Gupta.

"No Mom, you always stay two steps ahead. It was my first date with her, how could I?" answered Rohan.

"What did you talk about?" asked Mr. Gupta.

"Nothing much. I just met Ankita and she asked for some time," replied Rohan.

"But it would indeed be a wonderful surprise if she says yes," suggested Mr Gupta.

"I know what her answer would be," thought Rohan.

CHAPTER SEVEN

Same Day @ Ankita Home

Ankita was having lunch with her mom after her first date with Rohan. She asked her mother, "Maa, what do you know about Rohan? Is he a good match for me?"

"Have you analysed all the details about Rohan? Do you know everything about him?" Ankita further added questions to her list.

Her mother teased her, "Your first meeting made you Mrs. Lawyer. You came with a list of questions as a lawyer."

"Maa, I am feeling hungry. Please let me finish my food first."

"You are ignoring me, Ankita."

"Mom, you know me better."

"Let me discuss with Mrs. Gupta to come in the evening to settle the date for marriage."

"Mom, it's too early."

Ankita's Mom dialed Rohan's number.

It's ringing.

Rohan picked up the phone.

"Hi, Shalini this side. I wanted to invite you in the evening if you have time for today. Rohan handed over the phone to his mom to talk with Ankita's Mom.

He was standing close to his mother intending to hear their conversation.

He was whispering in his mother's ear, "Did she say 'YES'?"

He hugged his mom tightly. His mom said okay for the evening meeting.

Everything went as per Rohan's plan. He was happy and excited to meet her again and congratulate her.

Rohan's family came to Ankita's home in the evening. They had tea with snacks and started the discussion about their children's wedding. They decided on the final marriage date after ten days. Both families congratulated each other. Ankita and Rohan gave their views that it would be too early and this would be a rushy affair.

Their parents decided that we would plan together and it would not be any problem when they all were together. Rohan and Ankita decided to start shopping early.

Rohan requested Ankita to keep her second half free for one week so they could go shopping. They decided that Rohan would pick her from the hospital after her OPD Timings. If she had an emergency, then she could allocate her duties to Dr. Ishaan as she did last time. Ankita's mom was shocked to hear the name Ishaan.

"We will plan if we need any help from Ishaan or not," Rohan suggested.

"We decided everything together; the wedding planner kind of tasks, banquet hall, etc."

The next afternoon, Rohan came to the hospital and picked Ankita for shopping. They went to various malls to have an idea about the trends going on. Ankita got a call from the hospital to attend an emergency.

"You should call Ishaan to attend the patient," Rohan suggested.

"I know what I should do but he's on leave for today. I have to go," Ankita replied arrogantly.

Rohan decided to drop her at the hospital when they entered the parking lot, Rohan saw Ishaan with his friend in the parking lot.

"Hey, Ankita! Think of the devil and the devil comes," joked Rohan.

"What do you mean?" asked Ankita.

"Here is Dr. Ishaan," Rohan gestured.

"Stop this Rohan, he is on leave and with his friend."

Dr. Ishaan came towards Ankita.

"Hi, Ankita, meet my friend, Mehak," Ishaan introduced Mehak.

Rohan offered a gentle handshake to Ishaan and replied, "Hi, I am Rohan, Ankita's fiancé."

Ishaan was shocked to see him.

"Our marriage is scheduled after 10 days. So, we were supposed to be here for shopping, but an emergency at the hospital cancelled our plans. We will plan some other day," Rohan continued.

"You should take a day off for this, Ankita," Ishaan and Rohan spoke together.

"Don't waste time here Rohan, let's go, it's an emergency in the hospital. We should move fast," Ankita continued.

Rohan dropped her at the hospital and left for his house.

The whole day went in the hospital. Due to a lot of pending work to complete before marriage, the next day, Ankita took a day off from the hospital.

After having dinner with her mom; she went to her room; started a chat with Rohan and after almost one hour chat; they created a to-do list for tomorrow. But suddenly, Rohan suggested that why don't they start their day with a movie at PVR.

CHAPTER EIGHT

Next Day

In the morning, Rohan texted Ankita, "Good Morning Dear, see you soon."

Ankita texted him back, "Good Morning, we will meet around 9:00 a.m. sharp. I will be ready at that time; just pick me from the gate."

While having breakfast with mom, Ankita discussed all the minor details with her mom as she used to do that. Her mother was her only friend in this beautiful world. She always supported her in every walk of her life. As they were just discussing with each other, Ankita got a call from Rohan.

"Are you ready, Mam?" Rohan asked with curiosity.

Ankita hugged her mom; picked her white leather shoulder bag and moved towards the lift of the building.

"Yes, wait I am coming," Ankita replied sweetly.

Rohan and Ankita went shopping, but Rohan planned to go for a movie first. They bought tickets at the ticket counter for the show and went inside the PVR. They checked their seat number and relaxed at their seats to enjoy the movie. In the interval, when the lights of the hall switched on, they both saw Ishaan and his friend Mehak in the same movie hall. As the show was over, Ankita was feeling nervous. Rohan asked her repeatedly the reason behind her nervousness, but every time she started a new talk with a new topic.

Rohan thought for a while and suggested, "Let's go for a long drive as I want to share something with you."

Ankita got nervous again.

"Don't worry I am not going to break your heart; just a casual drive. I wanted to be with you. If you feel comfortable then only, we would plan. Otherwise, no issue."

They purchased all the accessories they planned for the day. After their shopping, they went to the parking lot with their shopping bags. They went for a long drive as Rohan wanted to change her mood. But she was still nervous as Rohan was in a very romantic mood.

"Please Ankita, share something if you want to," Rohan questioned her.

After a long drive, they stopped at a coffee shop for some change. At the coffee shop when Rohan tried to hold her hand, she resisted him to do so. Rohan tried his best to know the reason behind her awkward behaviour. But Ankita was in a dilemma.

How would Rohan react if she shared her past with Rohan?

After the coffee, they went back to their home. Ankita was changed a lot from morning to evening. She picked her shopping bags and waved to Rohan gently.

But after some struggle with her mind, she made a video call to Rohan to narrate the story behind her nervousness. She took a deep sigh and started her conversation, "Rohan, I know you are feeling upset with my awkward behaviour so let me share my pain with you. I and Ishaan were cool friends in the hospital. I appointed him as an intern in the hospital. I was impressed by his charming king-like personality. I assumed him as the prince of my dreams."

Rohan was listening very patiently and was feeling the way she had felt before.

Ankita continued her story, "But, suddenly everything changed when his parents rejected me as I have been staying with my mom only. When they got to know the story of my parents, they straightforward declined the proposal of our marriage. Ishaan's parents forced him to leave me and the job from that hospital as I am not of his kind. But Ishaan accepted only one condition as he would leave me but not the job from the hospital. His parents used to convince him that my mom and I belong to one particular society and culture and I will never adjust to that. So, Ishaan finally declared a break up of our five-year long friendship."

Rohan was listening calmly but Ankita was expecting something opposite to that. He consoled her to leave her past as bad weather.

He assured her, "I am always with you, as you are my first crush and love at first sight. But Ishaan was your crush only. How can I let you go in pain for the person who doesn't matter to you?"

Rohan assured Ankita to feel comfortable in his company as he would never allow anyone to hurt her again.

"Thank you, Rohan," she sighed deeply.

"I am lucky to have you as my life partner," confessed Ankita.

"How only you could be lucky, even though I am the luckiest person in the world to have a beautiful, lovely and caring partner!"

"Let me decide one thing before our marriage." Rohan put a condition. Ankita was shocked again.

Ankita asked, "What??"

Rohan smiled and continued, "Ankita, promise me."

"What promise, Rohan??"

"The only promise I want from you is to be best friends before our husband-wife relation."

Ankita smiled and nodded her head.

Ankita's mother called her for dinner. So, she requested to hold this conversation for half an hour.

"I have to go for dinner, else mom will come with food in my room."

"May I join you two lovely ladies at dinner?" asked Rohan.

"Please, not now," she smiled and disconnected his call.

CHAPTER NINE

Next Day

Rohan called Ishaan to meet him at the coffee house. As decided, they met at the coffee shop in the middle of the Sector–22 market around 5:30 p.m. They both shook hands and walked inside the coffee house to look for the empty chairs. After a few seconds, they got two chairs to sit in and ordered their coffee.

Ishaan asked, "Anything special, you called me suddenly."

Rohan warned Ishaan, "Stay away from Ankita as you have hurt her a lot. But remember now she is my life; nobody dares hurt her again otherwise I will forget that you were my friend before."

Ishaan explained about the relationship of Ankita's mom as she is a child of her father and mother's live-in relationship, but that never got acceptance in society.

"Then what?" Rohan wondered.

"Everyone has a right to love. It was their decision but that doesn't mean you will make Ankita realise that she will never get acceptance in society."

Rohan warned Ishaan, "Leave Ankita as she is the queen of my dreams. I would not allow you to shatter my dream and my dream girl Ankita."

Ishaan concluded his talk by informing his marriage plans and confessed, "I will never come in between you two."

Then Ishaan stood up from the chair and moved towards the door to leave the coffee house.

As Ishaan left the coffee house, the waiter served the two cups of coffee. Rohan ordered the waiter to bring the bill as he is in a hurry.

Rohan paid the bill; sat in his car and went to Ankita's hospital.

Rohan went to the receptionist and asked about Ankita. She was standing outside her cabin and asking Ishaan about his appointments and emergencies as he was taking a second half off.

Rohan was surprised to see Ishaan with Ankita and he went to Ishaan and warned, "How dare you talk to her?" The hospital staff was shocked, even Ankita was shocked at Rohan's reaction. Rohan held her arm and took her inside the cabin to tell her that she should not talk to Ishaan.

"Stop! Stop! It's not like that, Rohan. Please don't overthink and assume anything about Ishaan. He is taking a half-day off so I was discussing with him about his appointments," Ankita informed.

"Sorry as I went beyond my limits. Today I met Ishaan at a coffee house. Ishaan told me that he would not meet you again. Please stay relaxed and focus on our future and leave your past behind," Rohan assured.

"But I was only discussing our professional duties as he was taking half day leave. I am sorry if you assumed something else. That's it," explained Ankita.

CHAPTER TEN

The Next Day

Shalini woke up and started writing her diary as usual. Finishing her diary, she went to the kitchen to prepare tea. After putting the newspaper on the tray, she went to Ankita's room to wake her up. She pulled the curtains.

"Good morning Ankita!"

"Wake Up!"

"It's Morning!"

"Morning tea is here..."

"Mumma, please let me sleep for more."

"Get up, it's already 8:00 a.m. You will be late for the hospital."

"Mumma, I've already taken leave for two days for shopping."

"Then, won't you get ready to go shopping?" asked Shalini.

After having tea, Ankita again felt sleepy and lied on the bed and pulled the sheet over her face.

"What happened to you, Ankita?"

"It's 8:30 a.m. now."

"Mumma, please let me sleep for half an hour more as he will pick me around 10:00 a.m."

"Mumma just prepare the breakfast and I'll be there by that time."

"Okay, take rest."

"Have you decided what to wear?"

"Mumma, please keep some casual wear ready for me."

"What colour do you want to wear?"

"Any colour, Mumma. Choose yourself."

"Look, I've picked Grey kurta with Green leggings."

"Mummaaaaa...... Do you think I can sleep in such a nuisance?"

Shalini slammed the door and walked out towards the kitchen.

Ankita yelled in anger, "Enough Mumma. I think you won't let me sleep."

Ankita just closed her eyes when her phone rang.

"It's the worst day of my life," Ankita thought and picked up the phone with closed eyes.

"Hello. Who's this?"

"It's me, Rohan."

"Who's Rohan?"

"What happened Ankita? Are you okay? Good morning!"

"Oh, it's you. A very good morning."

"What do you mean 'it's you'?"

"Were you expecting someone else?"

"If I'm not mistaken, then we have planned for shopping today."

"Yes, yes, I know."

"Are you ready?"

"No, I'm still in the bed trying to sleep more for the last 15 minutes."

"What did you do the last night? Didn't you sleep?"

"Arre...... Nothing like that."

"I think Mr Lawyer you don't know the feeling of morning sleep."

"Oh, now I came to know my would-be Mrs Lawyer loves to sleep in the morning."

"I am going to disconnect the call to sleep peacefully. You two have destroyed my sleep."

"Two????"

"Who was the first one?"

"Rohan, please stop these questions. I want to sleep. We will discuss this once we meet."

"Ok Madam, just sleep till 9:30 a.m."

"I will call you then, Good Night," Rohan laughed gently.

Rohan started watching action movie trailers till 9:30 a.m.

As the clock stuck at 9:30 a.m, he called Ankita again, but she didn't pick the phone.

He tried again but he got the same message again, "The person you are trying to call is not answering, please try again later."

CHAPTER ELEVEN

Next Scene @ 10:00 a.m.

Ankita came out from the bathroom and was crying, "I am late. I am late. Oh My God! I shouldn't have slept."

She combed her hair and got ready to go with Rohan. She started calling her mom hurriedly, "Mom, I'm getting late and feeling hungry. Give me something to eat."

As she entered the kitchen, she was surprised as her mom was not in the kitchen.

"Ankita, I'm in the drawing-room. Come and have breakfast here with us."

"Us????"

She was surprised to see Rohan sipping tea in the drawing-room with her mom.

"Good morning, Ankita, 9:30 ho gaye kya???" taunted Rohan.

Ankita smiled gently and apologised, "So, Sorry!!"

They all had breakfast together and started sipping tea.

Ankita went to her room to pick her sling bag and left for shopping with Rohan.

They went to the elevator, hit the down button and started talking about their plans for shopping.

"We will start from VR Mall where we went earlier for the movie," Ankita suggested.

"Sure, Madam."

They reached near to the car; Rohan gently opened the door for Ankita.

"Thanks, Rohan."

She sat in the car, kept her mobile in the car front dashboard and wore the seat belt.

Rohan turned on the car stereo but Ankita wanted to sit in quiet so she turned it off.

"Do you want pin-drop silence in the car???? I hate peace."

"I am a peace-loving person."

"Oh My God! Two opposite personalities are going to mingle. Let's see what happens."

Ankita laughed.

"Thank God! I'm glad to hear your laughter."

They reached VR Mall and parked their car in parking lot A.

They went to a shop where they found beautiful costumes for their marriage. They took trials and decided the final costumes for their marriage ceremony. They both bought their wedding costumes from VR Mall. It took around more than an hour to finalise their wedding costumes. They gave them to alter these dresses as per their size.

They both ate ice cream as it was a hot summer afternoon.

Then they decided to go for antique and pearl jewellery shopping together as per the design of their dresses. Ankita found the jewellery very pretty and she bought two sets of jewellery too.

It was 3:30 p.m. Ankita and Rohan were sitting in a restaurant for Lunch. Ankita dropped a message to her mom and texted her that she was having lunch with Rohan at a restaurant.

After having lunch, Rohan dropped Ankita at her house around 4:45 p.m.

"Enjoyed the lunch with Rohan?" asked Shalini.

"Mom, you know. It was fun shopping. We ate ice cream; bought wedding costumes and jewellery also," replied Ankita.

"Wonderful! Now hurry up. Change your clothes and look what I purchased for you?" Shalini told Ankita.

"Mom, are you finished with your lunch?" asked Ankita.

"Yes, Beta," replied Shalini.

Give me two minutes to change, I want to show you the shopping we did today.

Shalini picked her shopping bags from the cupboard and arranged those bags on the bed.

Ankita came in her pink coloured T-shirt. She was looking princess in the same way it was written on her T-shirt.

She hugged her mom tightly and murmured in her mom's ears softly, "I love you maa."

They discussed their shopping for 30 minutes and a lot of other related crucial things. Ankita settled the shopping bags into one of the room's cupboards.

"Mom, I am really tired so wanna sleep for a while as you and Rohan disturbed a lot in the morning."

Ankita went to her room to take a power nap.

CHAPTER TWELVE

The Next Day

Both families decided to meet and started discussing the wedding preparations as the wedding was three days away.

Rohan and Ankita spent these days together. Every day they had a new plan.

Their marriage was on Monday. It was Friday morning. Ankita's family and Rohan's family went to meet the wedding planner. There they met Ishaan with his family. Ishaan's family was also discussing Ishaan's wedding.

Ankita suggested that they should go to some other wedding planner. Rohan advised, "We should concentrate on our work and they should concentrate on their work."

"Right, Rohan," replied Ms Shalini.

Finally, they booked the same wedding planner for their marriage whom Ishaan had selected for his marriage. They were feeling relaxed as now onwards, their wedding planner was going to handle all the preparations of their marriage.

The next day, they planned to go to the Golden Temple on a one-day trip. They started their journey around 6 a.m. and it took around 4 hours to reach Amritsar. They went there to take blessings from the Almighty as they were entering a new phase of their life. The whole day went in the Journey from Chandigarh to Amritsar. They came back around 8 p.m. They were very tired and had dinner on their way. The day was so hectic that they slept as they went to bed. They woke up as their alarm rang; exchanged good morning texts with each other and got ready for their remaining shopping.

CHAPTER THIRTEEN

Day of Mehndi & Haldi Ceremony

The wedding planner planned everything yellow as the theme of the mehndi ceremony. Everything was decorated with yellow colours like flowers, frills and curtains. All the dear ones were suggested to wear yellow dresses as well. Female guests were coming in yellow dresses with unique designs. Not only women but men were also there in sherwani, kurta with yellow jackets. The mehndi pandal was filled with yellow colour.

Ankita wore a yellow crop top and multi colour banarasi skirt with dupatta draped on her right shoulder. She was dressed with beautiful yellow-coloured original flowers jewellery. She was looking like an angel from heaven and ready to enter Rohan's world of love.

Rohan was dressed up with yellow sherwani with light cream colour legging and embroidered silk stole. He was looking like a perfect groom for Ankita. The mehndi ceremony was organised in the park of Ankita's apartment. All the guests were assembled in the park and were waiting for Ankita to come. As Ankita entered the mehndi pandal; suddenly DJ started playing the songs of mehndi and the ambience was filled up with enthusiasm. The ceremony was about to start. All her friends were on the dance floor. All the relatives started applying haldi to Ankita and blessed her for her wedding life. Turn by turn, all applied haldi to Ankita and started settling on the chairs arranged in the pandal.

As slowly by the time the relatives started having dinner and dispersed to their place as the ceremony was about to finish. All congratulated Ankita and Shalini for the ceremony.

CHAPTER FOURTEEN

Wedding Day

Finally, the day came of their uniting for what they were waiting for. The ambience was full of emotions.

'Din Shagna Da Chadya Aao Sakhiyon Ni Vehra Sajya' a famous wedding song from the film Phillauri mesmerised all the guests as they were joining in the wedding hall decorated with white and pink roses with illumination effects. The ambience of the wedding hall changed in the blink of an eye.

Laavan Resort was booked exactly seven days before the wedding as everything was happening on short notice. It was located out of the city crowd on the Landran-Sirhind highway. The resort has ample parking space and every guest was shocked to see the valet parking. The wedding hall was so spacious that even after the presence of thousands of guests, ample space for more to accommodate. The resort was decorated beautifully with white flowers with pink frills. The wedding planner left no stone unturned as planned every minute detail so well, the guests were surprised to see the arrangements.

The seating arrangement was so awesome that guests were busy taking selfies with the decoration. All were mesmerised to see the colour combination for the decoration. The colour theme was pink and white. White chairs with light pink frills were arranged beautifully to accommodate all the guests. All the guests were welcomed with the stick of red roses. The welcome ceremony at the resort widened the eyes and smiles of all the guests. All were served with welcome juices and snacks.

Around 10 p.m. the couple entered with the Military Band. The cameramen started following the couple to grab glimpses of the newlywed couple, the near and dear ones started taking pics of the couple on their phones as they were marching towards the stage of the hall.

The wedding ceremony was going in full swing. Suddenly Ishaan came with her friend Mehak and created a scene there. Then Shalini and Mehak tried to calm down all the situation. Mehak did her best to keep him away from Ankita's wedding ceremony. As the ceremony was over, Shalini got a unique connection with Mehak.

CHAPTER FIFTEEN

A New Friendship

A unique fragrance of Mehak impressed Shalini. They became their best friends in no time; their connection with their deep feelings grew deeper day by day. They planned every evening together. Their age gap never mattered in their friendship; they captured their beautiful moments. They spent their weekend in malls shopping as Rohan and Ankita were on their honeymoon, Mehak gave no chance to Shalini to feel lonely and sad. After five days when Rohan and Ankita came from their honeymoon, both Shalini and Mehak went to the Mohali Airport to receive them.

They reached the airport with a red rose bouquet to welcome the newly-wed couple. Rohan and Ankita came to the arrival terminal with their luggage trolley. Ankita was looking like a beautiful doll holding her shoulder bag on one side and clasping Rohan's arm.

Ankita hugged her mother so tight that her mother couldn't control her emotions; tears rolled down from her eyes. Mehak suppressed Shalini from the back and comforted her to control.

Ankita was surprised to see Mehak with her mom.

"Mehak, Why are you here with my mom?"

"What are you doing with my mom?"

Shalini calmed her daughter and told Ankita listen to her part first.

As they were going to sit in the cars, Mehak received a message from her father and she was surprised that the flight of her father was going to land within half an hour at the same Airport.

Mehak informed Shalini, "You all just leave as I have to stay here to welcome my father. He will be here exactly after thirty minutes."

"I will meet you at your place and will have lunch together," Mehak spoke and hugged her tightly.

Shalini invited Mehak and his father for lunch after his flight landed at the Mohali Airport.

"You all just go and relax for a while," Mehak enjoined her friend Shalini.

They put all their luggage in the car dicky and sat in the car. Rohan drove the car to Shalini's home. Ankita sat in the rear seat. Shalini sat in the centre seat and started surfing her mobile and asking about their travel.

Ankita kept quiet in the car but bombarded a series of questions to her mom once they reached home.

"Why was Mehak with you at the Airport?"

"What she wanted from you?"

"Maybe it was the plan of that selfish Ishaan?" Ankita continued without taking any pause.

"Oh! Just look at you, now who came with Rohan, it's not my daughter now you have become a lawyer as well," Shalini interrupted Ankita.

Rohan laughed cheerily. Rohan also questioned the presence of Mehak.

"She is just a friend," replied Shalini.

"But she is the friend of Ishaan too." Rohan and Ankita spoke and laughed together.

Ankita reacted weirdly, "Why has Ishaan allowed her friend to meet you? Don't you think he might have made a plan against us?"

Shalini and Rohan convinced Ankita not to think so far when there was nothing as she was thinking.

CHAPTER SIXTEEN

The Scene at the Airport

Mehak was busy surfing on her mobile as her father called her, "Mehak beta."

She turned; hugged her father and started fighting with her father about why he didn't inform her before so she could plan some surprise for him. She talked about her new friend, and requested him to come along with her to lunch at their home.

"I was at the airport to welcome Ankita and Rohan when I received your message," Mehak described.

Mehak called a cab to the Airport. Mehak helped her father to keep his suitcase in the dicky. Then they both sat inside and went to Shalini's home.

The cab driver stopped the car at Shalini's home. They came out of the cab; took the suitcase out from dicky and went inside the lift.

Mehak pressed the 8th-floor button as Shalini lived on the eighth floor. When the lift stopped on the 8thfloor, they came out with their luggage. Mehak's fathersaw the nameplate at the door and it was written 'Shalini Mehra and Dr. Ankita.' Mehak's father went in his old memories.

He shared, "I also knew one girl named Shalini who was my friend, but due to some family reasons I couldn't fulfil my promise to marry her."

Mehak recalled that story of her father and laughed, "She is still in your mind even after 25 years."

She continued to speak, "She is my best friend, not yours."

Time looked like it stopped for a while.

Mehak held her father's hand and pressed the bell at the door.

"Ding Dong"

Sheela opened the door and Mehak asked about Shalini.

Sheela informed her, "They all are in the bedroom and taking rest. You just settle in the drawing-room. I am calling them."

As Shalini heard the sweet voice of Mehak, she came while mentioning, "Oh! Mehak, we missed you a lot. Let's have lunch together."

But when Shalini entered the drawing-room, Mehak was sitting in front of her father. As Shalini went to sit on the sofa with Mehak, she just shouted at the person sitting on the adjoining sofa in the drawing-room.

"You? Anish. After 25 years."

"How did you get to know about me?"

"Why have you come now?"

"What you wanted from me?" Shalini bombarded Anish with questions.

"Shalini! He's my father," exclaimed Mehak.

"OMG! This was the person behind your half love story." Mehak exclaimed again.

Nobody could imagine how God was trying his best to complete this incomplete love story; how He was tying Shalini with Anish. God had finally brought the 25-year-old love story back from the past in front of Shalini.

After hearing the sounds from the drawing-room, Ankita and Rohan rushed out of the bedroom; moved towards the drawing-room, and asked about the person. At the same time, Sheela was observing the situation.

Ankita asked, "Mom, who is this person? Why are you yelling at him?"

Shalini replied, "He is Anish about whom I told you earlier."

Ankita was surprised as well as angry as she never expected him to come here.

Ankita shouted, "How dare you enter our house?"

She further added, "Mom, please tell him to go."

Anish was surprised to see Ankita. Anish exclaimed, "I am very happy to see you, beta."

Ankita replied, "You would have been happy when you left my mother."

"Mom, is he Mehak's father?" asked Ankita.

"Yes," replied Shalini.

"Mom, you told me that Mehak is your best friend. Then how you didn't know about her father?" asked Ankita.

"I told you that it was Ishaan's plan. He wanted to create misunderstandings in our life. You told me that Mehak is not like him," Ankita spoke angrily.

She went to her room; locked herself in the room and started crying. Shalini ran after her.

"Ankita, What's wrong with you? Why have you locked yourself in the room?" asked Shalini.

"Just tell him to go," replied Ankita in a low voice.

Mehak came after them and requested, "Please Shalini, don't assume me wrong. I am not taking his side. I just want you to listen to his part as well. Rest is up to you."

"Mehak, what he wants to say now?" shouted Shalini.

Rohan requested all to stay calm and go to the drawing-room so that he can convince Ankita to calm down. Mehak and Shalini went to the drawing-room.

After 15 minutes, when Ankita came, she screamed, "He is still here. Such an insensitive person you are"

"Please, don't judge a book by its cover," requested Mehak.

Anish explained, "Beta, when my parents got to know about Shalini, they told me to leave her as they would never allow me to leave Rajasthan, and Shalini's parents never allowed her to leave Mumbai."

"You should have told your parents that you love my mom," suggested Ankita.

Anish further explained his story, "Time was gone. When I came home one day my parents had fixed my marriage with a girl. I couldn't dare to speak or do something. Mehak's mom died as she delivered her."

"With a blink of an eye, my life was totally upside down. As were my deeds; so is my destiny. No one can understand my pain," Anish concluded.

"I am not interested in any of your stories," Ankita spoke furiously.

Shalini requested Mehak, "Please leave right now. Mehak! I never expected this from you."

Mehak was unable to explain her part as Shalini was not in a situation to understand her.

Sheela requested, "Please have lunch."

Mehak replied, "Sheela not this time maybe some other day."

"Very confident, Mehak! Are you sure I will allow you to enter my home next time?" exclaimed Ankita.

"Ankita, don't cross your limits," Shalini warned.

"Dad, I think we should leave," suggested Mehak.

"Very right, Mehak," Ankita taunted.

"Stop it, Ankita!" screamed Shalini.

Mehak left the house without noticing her father. She was thinking, "Why didn't dad go against his parents to accept Shalini?"

She just forgot that her father was still at Shalini's home.

Shalini called Mehak on the phone, "Where are you right now, don't run away from this awkward situation. It is a very sensitive matter so I think we should discuss this matter with patience by tomorrow. I know all this happened before your birth then how could I blame you for this? I request you to please calm down and come back to my place dear. How can I let you go without having lunch?"

After a few minutes, Mehak agreed to come.

Mehak again knocked on the door; Sheela opened the door and made her sit on the dining table for lunch. Rohan somehow convinced Ankita not to create any scene now. After all, she is mom's friend beside Ishaan's friend and daughter of Anish.

Ankita again got up from the chair; was about to leave when Rohan held her hand to make her sit. She still did not agree with her mom's words.

Then finally, Shalini warned Ankita, "Ankita! Don't create a scene at this time. Just have lunch and we'll discuss the matter afterward."

"I am sorry, Mehak," Shalini apologised for Ankita's behaviour.

"Don't worry, Shalini. I would have reacted the same way if I would be at her place. So, I can understand her feelings about you," replied Mehak.

"Let's have lunch and not discuss this matter right now," commanded Shalini.

Shalini asked Sheela to serve lunch to everyone. When Sheela was about to serve, Ankita got up from the chair and informed, "I am not in a mood to eat at the dining table.

Sheela, please bring my lunch to my room."

"Sure, Mam," replied Sheela.

Shalini was staring at Ankita as the latter was still against Mehak.

She asked, "Ankita, don't you think eating with everyone is a good idea? You are stretching this matter to a great extent. We will resolve it after lunch. So, please cooperate with us and have lunch with us."

As everyone had lunch; they got up; moved towards the drawing-room and settled there.

Shalini ordered Sheela to clear the dining table and prepare tea for everyone.

Mehak started, "Shalini, I never imagined that our relationship will change all of a sudden."

"No Mehak, our relationship has not changed and will never change. We will remain friends forever. You were with me when I was all alone. I will be grateful to God that he sent you to me as the best buddy of my life like Ankita," explained Shalini.

Ankita raised her eyebrows and was staring at her mom trying to know the reason behind her words.

Anish explained, "I never imagined that my daughter Mehak and Shalini would create such a great bond of friendship in a small period which I could not even do twenty–five years ago due to some unavoidable reasons. I am extremely sorry. I am still there to break your heart and your family. I don't know why God has given the same situation again and again. What does he want me to do now? I had not even thought in my dream that I would face you again. It is just like the earth is revolving so is our relationship. Now tell me Shalini, what would you have done if you were at my place. This meeting has created a crack between both the families."

"Stop it, Dad! Why are you saying a crack in both the families? We all are one family if we try. I know adjustments will take time."

"Mehak, you are crossing your limits. We all need time to make the decision. Time has changed, a lot of things have changed as well. I don't think it would work now. Please give all of us some time to think," replied Shalini.

"I am not in a hurry. I am just giving my views. Why can't we become one family rather than a split one?" informed Mehak.

"You're right at your place. But you should think about all of us. The most important thing in a family is the connection. But, do you think that Ankita will accept you and your father? Never, then why you want both the families to unite," Shalini replied.

"Very right, mom. I will never accept Mehak and her father. So, please let them go. I can't tolerate them anymore," Ankita explained her perspective.

"Ankita, I know what you are feeling about me. I too think you are right but please understand if both the families unite then we can live happily," replied Mehak.

Ankita explained to her, "I don't think these two families can live happily ever after they unite. There is no possibility so I don't think we should try."

"I think we should go back home. I can't talk about this matter now. So, we should move now, Rohan?" asked Ankita.

"Sure, Ankita," replied Rohan and he assured Shalini to give Ankita some time to understand everyone's point of view. They went back home.

CHAPTER SEVENTEEN

Another Scene

Rohan and Ankita went into their bedroom with their luggage. They unpacked their luggage. Ankita was whispering a lot while unpacking her luggage.

"Calm down, Ankita," Rohan suggested.

"How could I?"

"All of this happened with a blink of an eye," replied Ankita.

"Be mature; try to understand, Ankita. Mom has not said anything in favour or against Mehak and her father. She needs your as well as her time to think that's why she didn't give any consent to them."

"Rohan, if she didn't favour anyone then why she stopped me from speaking against Mehak. She favoured Mehak."

"Ankita, the reason is that you are reacting too much, that's why your mom stopped you from giving a bad impression in front of everybody. Though she stopped you many times, you still behaved awkwardly."

"Rohan, I reacted awkwardly?"

"I knew that it was Mehak's plan – first to become friend and then bring her father to our home for creating a scene at home and spoiling our lives."

"No Ankita, nothing like this. Please, stop it. It is just your imagination, nothing real. If she knew that his father was your mom's past then she could have created a scene when we were away. You should believe Mehak and give her a chance to explain her point of view."

"I think you are favouring Mehak too. How can I believe her as she is Ishaan's friend too? I believed Ishaan and you know what he did. Now, I can't believe Mehak."

"Ankita, why do you always forget that Mehak is mom's best friend?"

"Ankita calm down, please."

"Why are you allowing someone to destroy our relations?"

"Can you see we are fighting like kids without any reason, please think logically?"

"Ok," sighed Ankita.

"Let's wait till tomorrow. Whatever mom will decide will be the best decision for all. We need to respect her feelings as it's her life." Rohan convinced Ankita and hugged her tightly.

"Let's sleep now, I am tired a lot after this drama."

CHAPTER EIGHTEEN

The Next Day

Shalini woke up and went to the balcony to see the rising sun and started praying that whatever happens for a good reason.

"God, please give me enough strength to make another good decision in my life. Every morning when I get up, I love to start my day with the habit of being stronger than before."

Shalini was wondering and thinking about her daughter. She started writing in her diary.

Suddenly, tears rolled down her eyes and made impression on her diary.

She folded her diary and hugged it tightly.

Silently, she was observing the situation and the after-effects of her decision.

"How will everyone react to my decision?"

Shalini called Ankita and Mehak to join her around 11:00 a.m. She was thinking about Ankita and Mehak and staring at the clock as her heart was beating faster than the ticking sound of a clock.

When Ankita came, she was surprised to see Mehak sitting in the drawing-room and having tea with mom.

"Oh My God!! Mehak, you don't leave any chance to impress my mom. I know my mom is a beautiful soul on this planet but I will never allow you to take advantage of my mom's kind-heartedness," Ankita spoke furiously.

"Ankita, you started again. Please don't say anything," Shalini advised.

"Come and sit, Ankita. I want to tell you about my decision," Shalini stated.

Mehak and Ankita were thinking about Shalini's decision. All were curious to know her decision while having tea.

I thought a lot about this matter and finally decided not to lose Mehak. The happiness of Mehak had no bounds when Shalini said that she is sure about her decision.

"I don't want to lose my friend," Shalini holds Mehak's hands in her hands.

"I don't want to think about anyone except my daughter and my friend," Shalini expressed her feelings.

"Mom, Are you sure you want to be in friendship with Mehak after knowing about her?" Ankita questioned her mom.

"Yes Ankita, I am sure about my decision. She is not responsible for anything. I will never punish my friend who hasn't committed any mistake. But I will never accept Anish with you," concluded Shalini.

But I think I should inform dad about your decision. Shalini and Ankita both agreed with her decision.

Mehak called her father and informed him about Shalini's decision. All were tongue-tied watching her inquisitively. Shalini was observing the situation and was feeling relaxed after making the best decision of her life.

When someone leaves you, it doesn't mean that you are all alone. Just believe in the Almighty that He is sending someone special for you. So, what I have decided to do, I am sure it will make all of us happy.

Because I have a life to live and I need to live it in the best possible way. I don't want to live in the past that's why I have decided to move on. I want to live in my present and want to be a very strong and happy woman. Now onwards my life will be a great party for me and will live every moment with my best friend, Mehak.

"The decision of Shalini signifies her wish to have a friend and daughter together," Anish finally concluded.

"I need some time Mehak," Ankita requested Mehak.

"No problem Ankita. It's my pleasure that you have no problem with me."

Shalini sets to start freshly with her friend Mehak and her daughter Ankita. Patiently, months after months, years after years, she started her life again with Mehak for aspirations that were deeply pressed in her heart to explore the world and life with her.

Love is not the ultimate need of life.

"Sometimes all we need are supportive shoulders to cry on and to calm down and I found that in you, Mehak. Thanks a lot for being with me without any expectations and conditions," Shalini shared her feelings with Mehak.

"Friendship is a wonderful relationship," Mehak confessed.

I salute you Shalini. You are the strongest woman in the world I ever met.

"I know I am the strongest woman in the world as I have two supportive pillars Mehak and Ankita," Shalini said.

Shalini started writing in her diary how she quit like a strong woman and took the best decision of her life to choose friendship and quit her relationship of love.

Life is not always a bed of roses. All have to go through the various seasons of life. It was another season just like autumn, old relations swept away like old leaves and new relations sprouted with Mehak and she filled their lives with her unique fragrance of love and care...

About The Author

Ravinder Kaur is a homemaker turned author. She is an Indian novelist who writes fiction and nonfiction. She spends most of her time thinking about life and other philosophical matters, and she has been accused of thinking too much. Born and brought up in Ludhiana, she comes from a middle-class family and has wonderful life experiences. She lives in Kharar, Punjab with her beautiful family. She is a dotted mother of two lovely daughters. She feels ecstatic in the natural surrounding.

"Live Life as Your Last Inning" is her debut nonfiction intended to inspire everyone for a higher level, which everyone has put off for another day. 'Positive Alphabets of Life' is her second book intended to bring about a change in life. This book is a unique effort to change the perspective and give a new outlook to transform the world.

A Humble Appeal

I shall be grateful if you send your valuable feedback on any aspect of the book or any suggestions you may have in your mind. Please feel free to discuss.

You can submit your feedback by email on:
virdi.ravinder@yahoo.in

You can follow me on all the social media pages.
www.linktr.ee/AuthorRavinderKaur

Other Books

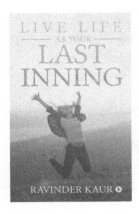 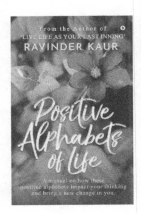

"Live Life As Your Last Inning" and "Positive Alphabets of Life" are available on Amazon, Flipkart, and Notion Press.

CPSIA information can be obtained
at www.ICGtesting.com
Printed in the USA
LVHW032026060223
738782LV00004B/938

9 781684 871155